Alice Savage

ELI'S COMING

Alice Savage grew up in a theatrical family and began writing plays in the fifth grade. As an English teacher of adult learners, she combines creative writing with a deep awareness of language to illuminate the worlds of immigrants and cultural explorers. She credits her multicultural family as inspiration. An author on many course books for Oxford University Press, Cambridge University Press, Pearson, and others, Alice has presented widely on the role of drama in language learning. She has published several award-winning one-act plays. Her dramatic fiction shows what happens when characters address challenges for which they may or may not be prepared. Alice lives in Houston.

First published by Gemma in 2025.

www.gemmamedia.org

©2025 by Alice Savage

Printed in the United States of America

978-1-956476-42-2

Library of Congress Cataloging-in-Publication Data

Names: Savage, Alice, 1962- author.
Title: Eli's coming / Alice Savage.
Other titles: Eli is coming
Boston : Gemma, 2025. | Series: Gemma open door
Identifiers: LCCN 2024056726 (print) | LCCN 2024056727
(ebook) | ISBN 9781956476422 (trade paperback) |
ISBN 9781956476439 (epub)
Subjects: LCGFT: High interest-low vocabulary books. | Novels.
Classification: LCC PS3619.A8286 E45 2025 (print) |
LCC PS3619.A8286 (ebook) | DDC 813/.6–dc23/eng/20241203
LC record available at https://lccn.loc.gov/2024056726
LC ebook record available at https://lccn.loc.gov/2024056727

Cover by Laura Shaw Design

Named after the brightest star in the Northern Crown, Gemma is a nonprofit organization that helps new readers acquire English language literacy skills with relevant, engaging books, eBooks, and audiobooks. Always original, never adapted, these stories introduce adults and young adults to the life-changing power of reading.

GEMMA

Open Door

To Erin Miller, a great teacher
and friend

TABLE OF CONTENTS

1. The Hair Salon

Olivia is sweeping the floor when the salon door opens.

"Hello? Anyone here?"

Olivia frowns. She knows that voice.

Adriana Bettencourt is standing in the doorway. She has red hair. She is wearing a purple dress with green shoes.

"Where's Monica?" Adriana says without looking up from her phone.

"She's traveling," says Olivia. "She'll be back next week."

"I need a haircut," says Adriana. "It's an emergency."

"I'm sorry," says Olivia. "Your hair looks nice." She tries to be helpful.

"No, it looks terrible."

"OK." Olivia waits.

"I guess you'll have to do it," says Adriana.

"Me?"

"Can you? I have a date tonight, and it's important."

"Now?"

"Yes. Please?"

Olivia does not want to, but she says "yes." Adriana has a dress shop down the street, and she knows Olivia's boss.

Adriana sits, and Olivia looks at her in the mirror. "So, what are we doing today?"

"I need a very straight cut, like Monica does," says Adriana. "Very straight."

"I'll do my best," says Olivia. She is nineteen, and customers often worry about her skills.

"I won't talk so you can focus," says Adriana after Olivia washes her hair. Then she starts talking. "So, I'm seeing a doctor," says Adriana. "He's taking me to a party."

"That's nice," says Olivia.

"I'm deciding on clothes. I hate black, but everyone wears black to these things."

"Do they?" Olivia asks politely.

"Yes." Adriana puts down her phone. "Black is easy, but I like colors."

"I wear colors," says Olivia. She looks down at her pink skirt.

"Good for you!" says Adriana. "I'm going to wear green. It looks good with my hair."

"Smart!" says Olivia. She puts her hands on Adriana's head to stop her from moving.

"What about you?" asks Adriana. "What's going on in your life?"

"Nothing," Olivia begins to cut.

"That's not true. Are you still seeing that boy, Skip?"

"Skip? No way. He moved." Olivia shakes her head.

Adriana looks at her in the mirror. "Is there someone new?"

Olivia's face feels hot. She cannot hide it.

"Oh, tell me! I promise I won't tell anyone," says Adriana.

Olivia does not believe her. Nineteenth Street is only four blocks long, but it has the salon, Adriana's dress shop, a bank, a shipping store, Shini's café, shops, and even a small hospital. Adriana talks *to* everyone *about* everyone.

"He's a college student," Olivia says. "He works at Shini's café."

"How exciting," says Adriana. "How did you meet?"

"He came in for a haircut."

"Perfect! Do I know him?"

"I don't think so. He's new in the neighborhood."

"Where is he from?

Olivia takes a deep breath. "Syria."

"Syria?"

"Yes," says Olivia.

"I know a woman from Syria. She works for me. Her name is Mona."

"That's Rashid's mother."

"You're dating Rashid?" Adriana sits up. Olivia stops cutting.

"What's wrong with that?" says Olivia.

"Nothing," says Adriana. "He was in the hospital."

"Well, yes. He got hit by a car."

"I know."

"You know everything, Ms. Bettencourt."

"I'm nosy. So, what does your mother think?"

"It doesn't matter." Olivia cuts again, but it is not straight. "It's my life."

"Of course it is," says Adriana. "But be careful."

"Why?"

"You know. Rashid is a nice kid, but . . ."

"But what?"

"Men from that part of the world can have certain . . . expectations."

Olivia frowns. "Well, where is your doctor from?"

"He's from Houston," says Adriana. "So much easier, same language and all."

She looks at Olivia in the mirror, but Olivia does not answer.

When Olivia finishes, Adriana looks at her hair. It is straight, but it is much shorter. Adriana frowns. She pays Olivia and leaves the shop.

Olivia starts to sweep up the red hair. Then her phone buzzes.

There is a text from her mother: *Make sure you are home for dinner. I have a surprise for you.*

Olivia texts back: *I can't. I have plans.*

Can you change them?

Olivia texts back: *No.*

With that boy?

Olivia texts back: *Yes, with Rashid.*

Olivia waits, but the phone is silent.

She shrugs and continues to clean.

2. Rashid's Big Night

Rashid is in the kitchen at Shini's café. Sunlight comes in through a high window. It shines on clean white walls. A pile of dark red tomatoes sits in front of him. He is cutting the tomatoes to make a cold soup.

"Do you have enough tomatoes?" Rashid's boss comes in the kitchen. Shini has short dark hair, and she is wearing black and white chef's pants.

Shini looks at the tomatoes. "We're going to need more. People love cold soup on a hot day." Shini puts salt on a tomato and takes a bite. "So good," she says.

Rashid does the same. The tomato is fresh and full of flavor.

"I'm going out for more tomatoes and fish," says Shini.

"We have fish," Rashid looks up.

"We need more. Two big parties are coming."

"Are you doing a fish special?"

"Yes, with greens."

"Oh, that's perfect for late summer."

"Are you going to be OK here?"

"Of course," says Rashid. He points to the tomatoes.

Rashid watches Shini leave. Then he goes to the dining room. He makes a coffee and adds sugar. He drinks it quickly. He washes the cup and puts it back. Shini does not allow workers to drink her expensive coffee, but he needs it.

Suddenly, there is a knock on the glass door. Rashid sees a tall woman in a blue T-shirt. It is Shini's girlfriend, Wren. Rashid lets her in.

"Caught you!" says Wren.

"No, you didn't," says Rashid. "You didn't see anything."

Wren smiles. "You just drank an espresso. I saw you! But don't worry. I won't tell Shini."

Rashid smiles. "You want one?"

"Sure," she says. Wren has light colored hair and green eyes. She takes the coffee and sits at the counter. "What's up?"

"I'm making tomato soup. Shini's at the market, buying fish."

Wren shakes her head. "I don't eat fish."

"I know. You're a vegetarian."

"Right."

"That's so hard!" says Rashid.

"Actually, it's easy," says Wren. "Do you know when she'll be back?" Rashid shrugs.

Wren drinks her coffee. "You look tired."

"I am. I didn't sleep last night."

"Here, I'll help you." Wren washes her cup and puts it away. Then she follows Rashid to the kitchen and takes out a cutting board.

"So why can't you sleep?" Wren bites into a tomato and closes her eyes. "Mmm," she says.

"No reason. I was just texting."

"Texting who?"

"Olivia."

"Olivia from the salon?"

"Yes, that's her."

"Good for you!" says Wren. "I like her."

"You know her?"

"Everyone knows everyone around here," says Wren. "I used to babysit Olivia."

"Funny, she babysits my nephews now," says Rashid.

"Well, don't break her heart," says Wren. "You and your big dark eyes. You could do a lot of damage."

"I'm not going to break her heart," says Rashid.

"You'd better not."

"No, I'm serious. I really like her. She makes me feel safe."

"That's a strange thing to say."

"Really? I just mean, when I'm with her, my bad thoughts go away."

"Oh, you mean like the war in Syria?" Wren takes a quick look at Rashid.

"Yes." Rashid looks sad for a moment. Then he smiles. "But Olivia thinks the world is a good place."

"Yeah, she's got a good spirit," says Wren.

They work quietly for a while. Then Shini returns with more tomatoes and two large silver fish. Her blue eyes light up when she sees Wren.

"You are just the person to brighten my day," she says. "I got three more calls. We are going to be very busy. Can you help out tonight?"

Wren nods. "Sure."

"And you?" Shini turns to Rashid. "I really need you tonight. One of the line cooks is sick. Can you stay?"

Rashid pauses.

"You can work the line," says Shini.

Rashid thinks for a moment. Shini is giving him an opportunity. He wants to be a chef, and he needs experience.

"Are you sure?"

"Yes, you can cook. Unless you want to keep making salads and washing dishes," says Shini.

"Well, OK," says Rashid. He will have to cancel his plans with Olivia.

"Good," says Shini. "Let's get started on those onions."

3. Change of Plans

Olivia goes home for lunch. She walks down Nineteenth Street, past the hospital, and onto the bike path. Then she turns on Summer Street. When she gets to her house, she sees her neighbor. Brita waves from the front porch of a small yellow house. It has a big yard, and there are trees for shade. Her three-year-old son Ethan and six-year-old son Kyle are playing in a small pool. Teddy from down the street is with them. The boys are wet and screaming.

Olivia waves back. Olivia likes Brita. Her neighbor has friendly blue eyes and a nice smile. Olivia spends a lot of time at the yellow house because

Rashid lives there. "Good day for a swim!" she says.

"I have to keep them busy," says Brita.

Olivia hears her name. She turns. Her mother is standing on the sidewalk.

"Do you know this car?" asks Jane. She is frowning at an old gray car.

"No, should I?"

"Maybe it belongs to your friends across the street," her mother points at Brita. "It's in front of my house. I need the space."

"It's not their car," says Olivia. "What are you doing home?"

"I'm just here for a few minutes." Jane turns and looks at the house. "A worker is coming to build a fence."

"Why?"

"We need one."

"OK, if you say so." Olivia looks at the two-story home. It is white with a red door and black trim. She can see two cats in the window.

"I'll feel better behind a fence." Jane opens the door, and they go in.

Olivia goes to the kitchen and opens the refrigerator. "I'm hungry."

"There's yogurt," says Jane.

"Is that all? Why don't we ever have real food?"

"Yogurt is real food. What do you want?"

"How about lamb?"

"Lamb? You like lamb now?"

"Sure, it's delicious with yellow rice. Rashid's mom makes it."

"Good for her," says Jane. "But I don't have time to cook."

Olivia finds some peanut butter and a banana. Her mother takes out a diet soda. They sit at the kitchen counter.

"What's the surprise?" Olivia opens the peanut butter and puts a spoon in.

"Oh, nothing," says her mother, smiling. "The Carters are coming for dinner."

"Skip's family?" Olivia drops the spoon.

"Yes, I wanted to surprise you."

Olivia carefully puts some peanut butter on the banana. She takes a bite.

"Well," says her mother smiling. "What do you think? Can you change your plans?"

Olivia does not answer. She points to her mouth. It takes a long time to eat.

"No," she says finally.

Jane frowns.

Olivia shakes her head. "Rashid and I are biking downtown to see some music."

"I'm sure he would understand if you told him one of your oldest friends is in town."

"My old boyfriend, you mean!" says Olivia. "I know you don't like Rashid."

"I don't have anything against him," says Jane. "But this is special. Skip's mom called, and she specifically said 'Wouldn't it be nice to get the kids together?'"

"Mom, Skip and I broke up."

"But only because they moved," says Jane. "Now they're back."

"Mom, I'm sorry, but I have plans."

Olivia's phone buzzes. She sees Rashid's photo and smiles. Then she reads the text, and her smile disappears.

"What is it?" Jane picks up Olivia's banana. She puts peanut butter on it and takes a bite.

"Rashid. He can't go out tonight. He has to work." Olivia puts down her phone.

"Well, that's perfect," Jane says. "You can eat with us. I'm ordering barbecue from Pinkerton's."

"That'll make Skip happy," says Olivia.

"I know," says her mother smiling. "Skip loves Pinkerton's."

"I've got to get back to work," says Olivia.

"What about your lunch?" says Jane.

"I'm not hungry anymore." Olivia gets up and goes to the door.

Jane turns on the radio. A storm is forming in the Atlantic Ocean. Jane shrugs and throws out Olivia's banana.

4. Dinner Rush

Rashid is outside the café. He is writing dinner specials on a blackboard. There is cold tomato soup for a starter. Then he writes "fresh fish with greens and rise." The dessert is a summer fruit tart. Rashid steps back and looks at his work.

"You spelled 'rice' wrong," says Wren coming up behind him. "It's with a *c* not an *s*."

Rashid rubs out "rise" and writes "rice." "There," he says.

"Yes, but it's messy," says Wren. "Let me do it."

"My writing is nicer."

"You think so?"

"Yes. I'll do it." He wipes off the board. He is starting over when Shini comes out.

"Hey, I need you guys in the kitchen!" she says.

"Just writing the specials," says Rashid.

"It doesn't take two people."

"It does," says Wren. "One to write and one to spell."

"Well, please hurry. Someone needs to wash the greens."

"OK," says Wren. She follows Shini inside. Rashid finishes writing. He sets the menu on the sidewalk and steps back. The restaurant looks lovely with baskets of flowers hanging over the outdoor tables. He would like to bring Olivia here.

On his way back to the kitchen, Rashid passes a couple sitting at the bar. "Yep, I'm getting worried," says the man. "Eli's a big one."

"Huge," says the woman, "and coming straight for us!"

Rashid looks around, but he does not see anyone. When he returns to the kitchen. Shini is at the counter. She points a knife at him.

"You've got a pepper steak," she says. "Don't overcook it!"

Rashid puts some oil in a pan. The pan is very hot. He drops a steak in. Then he throws cut carrots and squash in another pan. He shakes the vegetables, and they quickly turn brown. Rashid slides them onto a plate. He turns the steak over. When it is done, he sets the steak next to the vegetables. He pours cream and spices in the pan and finishes the sauce. Rashid pours the sauce over the steak and puts it in the window. There are already three more orders.

Shini is cooking fish now. "Hot, hot, hot!" she says. Then she puts two specials out.

"Ow," says Wren on the other side. She almost drops the plates.

"Careful," says Shini.

More orders come, and Rashid forgets about time. There is only the hot stove, the meat, vegetables, and endless white plates.

Shini works beside him. He feels nervous when she looks at him, but she does not say anything.

When the work finally slows down, Rashid pushes a piece of bread through some sauce in a pan and puts it in his mouth. Then he turns and leans against the stove.

"You're on fire!" says Shini.

"I know," says Rashid. "That was fast!"

Then Rashid feels something cold hit his back.

"Hey!" he yells. Water runs down his shirt and pants and into his shoes.

"What did you do that for?" he asks.

"You really *were* on fire," says Shini laughing. "I had to pour water on your shirt."

"Oh, I thought you were happy because I cooked so fast."

"I was. But you shouldn't lean against a stove."

Rashid feels his back. He has burn marks on his shirt, but he is not hurt.

Wren comes in from the dining room with one more order.

"They're all talking about Eli," she says.

"Eli is still a long way away," says Shini.

"Not that far away now," says Wren.

"Who is Eli?" asks Rashid.

"A storm," says Shini.

"It *was* a storm," Wren corrects Shini. "Eli is a hurricane now."

5. Skip

"What are you going to wear?" Jane is putting glasses and paper plates on the counter.

"What's wrong with this?" Olivia asks.

"Your shirt is dirty."

"No, it's not."

"Look," Jane points to a dark spot on Olivia's blue shirt.

"That's just a little hair color."

"You should change."

Olivia runs upstairs to her room. She opens her closet, but stops when she hears a car door open and close. She goes to the window and looks out. The Carters are outside. When she sees Skip climb out of the back seat, her heart beats a little faster. He is tall, and he looks a little heavier in a big shirt with long sleeves. His blond hair is shorter, but he is the same Skip.

Olivia smiles. She quickly changes her shirt and comes downstairs. Jane is hugging Mrs. Carter. Then she tells Skip he is looking good.

"Thank you," says Skip, "It's nice to see you again, Mrs. Hopper."

"I'm still a Hopper, but not a 'Mrs.,'" says Jane.

Skip looks at Olivia with nervous green eyes. "Hi," he says.

"Hi, Skip," says Olivia.

Jane invites everyone into the kitchen. The barbecue from Pinkerton's is on the counter. They fill paper plates with meat and potato salad. Then they sit around the glass table in the dining room.

"The Carters have been traveling," Jane tells Olivia.

"Oh, you could say that," says Mrs. Carter. "Most of it was work. Brad was doing a project in Denmark, but we did take a few weeks to see Paris and London."

"Wow," Olivia looks at Skip. "Was it amazing?"

"It was OK," he says. "Kind of like here, but everything is older and smaller and colder."

"I'd love to go there," says Olivia. "I want to see the museums and drink coffee in the cafés. It looks so beautiful."

"That's what people say," says Skip. "But Houston has museums and cafés. No need to get on a plane to drink coffee."

"But there's so much history." Olivia leans forward. "Tell me everything. Didn't people dress differently? What did they talk about?"

Skip shrugs. "People wear scarves and ride bicycles a lot. You'd like the biking."

"It was kind of cold, though," says Mrs. Carter. She looks at her husband. "I agree with Skip. I was glad to come home."

Jane lifts her diet soda. "We are happy to have you back!"

"We are happy to be back," says Mr. Carter. "And we have news."

"Skip is going to the University of Houston," Mrs. Carter interrupts her husband.

"Wow!" says Jane. "That's wonderful. Isn't it wonderful, Olivia?"

"Yes," says Olivia.

"He's in the business program."

"We're so proud of you, Skip!" says Jane.

"Mom did it," says Skip. "She filled out the application, wrote the essay, everything."

"I helped a little." Mrs. Carter smiles at Olivia. "But I didn't write the essay."

"Yes, you did!" says Skip.

"He's looking forward to the football games," interrupts Mr. Carter. "Aren't you, son?" He turns to Olivia. "I loved college football."

"Olivia is also thinking about U of H," Jane says.

"I am?" Olivia looks at her mother.

"You should think about business." Mr. Carter says. "It's easy. All you need is a personality."

Mrs. Carter puts her hand on her husband's arm. "Then I don't know how you keep a job."

Jane laughs, and Olivia nods politely. Then she looks at Skip. "Do you want to sit outside?"

Skip stands up quickly. "Sure!"

"That's a great idea," says Jane. "You two go out on the porch. You have a lot to talk about."

It is hot outside, and the insects are loud. Olivia sits on the steps. "It seemed like you wanted to get out of there," she says.

"I did. Thank you!" says Skip. "I love my parents, but they were driving me crazy." He sits next to her.

"Aren't you hot?" Olivia points to Skip's heavy shirt.

"No, I'm fine," says Skip. "I missed hot weather."

Olivia's cat, Winken, comes over to Skip, and he pets her.

"She remembers me," he says. Then he looks at Olivia. "I missed you."

Olivia does not answer. She moves away a little.

"Sorry," Skip says. "I've had a rough year."

"A rough year? You were in Europe! I would die for a trip like that."

"Hah!" says Skip.

"I thought you were having fun."

"Fun? My parents took me away from my friends and put me in a dark, gray city full of old buildings." He reaches for her hand. "All I wanted was home."

Olivia is quiet. She is looking at his arm.

"Oh, Skip," she says, looking at the long red cuts on his skin. "You're not OK, are you?"

It is not a question. She knows something is wrong, and she wants to help.

6. Nosy Neighbor

Miss Polly is sitting on her couch. The old woman has a cup of tea, and she is watching the weather on TV. Round white hurricane clouds are spinning toward the Texas coast. There is a small hole in the center. It is the eye of Hurricane Eli.

"It's getting closer," says the weather woman.

"I can see that!" Miss Polly tells the TV. Then she turns to her dog. "Don't worry, Tilly. I have water, dog food, and five cans of soup. We'll be fine!"

A car door closes, and Tilly starts barking. Miss Polly goes to the door. A truck is parked outside her house. She frowns. A man gets out and walks over to Jane's house.

Miss Polly goes outside and looks at the truck. She sees wood and tools in the back. "Oh great! Now there will be workers in my parking place!" Miss Polly is turning to go back inside when she hears voices next door. She moves closer to listen. It is Rashid, the Syrian boy with the dark eyes. Miss Polly likes Rashid, and he sounds upset.

"She was sitting with a guy," Rashid says.

"Did you recognize him?" asks Brita.

"No, I'd never seen him before, and they were holding hands."

"But you said it was dark. Are you sure?"

"Yes, I could tell when they stood up."

"Oh, that's strange."

"I know. I thought Olivia liked me."

"She does. She's here all the time, and I don't think it's to see me!" says Brita.

"Then she hugged him."

"Oh," Brita frowns. "Have you thought there's an explanation? Maybe he's her cousin."

"She's never talked about a cousin, and Americans don't hold hands with their cousins."

Miss Polly moves closer. Tilly barks, and Brita looks up.

"Hello, Miss Polly," Brita says.

"I'm just doing some yardwork," says Miss Polly pushing flowers to the side. "But I couldn't help it. I heard you."

Brita laughs.

"You have girlfriend problems," says Miss Polly.

"I don't have a girlfriend," says Rashid. "Not anymore."

"Did the boy have blond hair?"

"Yes."

"His name is Skip," says Miss Polly.

"Who is he?" asks Brita.

"He used to live in your house."

"Our house?" asks Brita.

"Yes. He grew up there. He used to throw balls in my yard and crush the flowers."

"I see," says Brita. "That's why you were worried about Kyle."

"Well, Kyle's a boy, too."

"But not all boys crush flowers,"

"Yes, yes, I know." Miss Polly turns to Rashid. "Skip was Olivia's boyfriend in high school."

"See!" says Rashid to Brita. "I knew they weren't cousins."

"What are you going to do about it?" asks Miss Polly.

"Nothing."

"Nothing?"

"What good would it do? If she wants to get back together with her boyfriend, it's her decision."

"Now just wait, Rashid," says Brita. "You should hear her story."

Just then, the door across the street opens. Jane comes out with the worker. They shake hands, and he leaves.

Brita is surprised when Jane walks over to chat.

"Ready for Eli?" Jane opens a can of diet soda.

"I have no idea. I've never been through a hurricane," says Brita.

"Are you leaving then?" Jane asks.

"We haven't decided," says Brita. "Are you?"

"Oh, yes," Jane takes a drink. "It's too hot when the electricity goes out, and I need my air conditioning. We would have left sooner, but some old friends are in town."

"Let me guess," says Miss Polly. "The Carters."

"Yes," says Jane. "You saw them." Then Jane smiles at Brita and Rashid. "You are living in the Carters' house. Their son Skip and Olivia grew up together."

"Oh, I see," says Brita.

"Skip and Olivia are very close." Jane smiles again.

Rashid frowns. He crosses his arms and looks away.

"That's nice," says Brita. She turns to Rashid. "Let's go, Rashid. We need to check on your mother. She's staying with Vincent's parents. Maybe they need help."

Jane and Miss Polly watch Brita and Rashid go in the yellow house. Then Miss Polly looks at Jane. "Hmm," she says.

"What did I say?" Jane asks.

"Nothing," says Miss Polly, "but your message was clear. You want Olivia to break up with Rashid and get back with Skip."

"Good," Jane drinks her soda. "It just makes sense. Olivia is happier with Skip."

"Maybe," says Miss Polly.

"Why do you say that?" asks Jane. "I thought you'd agree with me. Adriana does."

"Young people have their own ideas," says Miss Polly. "Now, if you'll excuse me. I've got to look for candles."

"Candles? You aren't leaving?" Jane is surprised.

"And miss all the fun?" Miss Polly smiles. "I *like* hurricanes."

7. The Wind

Rashid is in the yard with his uncle, Joe. They are looking at the yellow house when the neighbor comes by. Paco is a short, friendly man with dark hair and an easy smile. His wife Dolores is from Mexico.

"How are you doing?" says Joe.

"Taking some time off work," says Paco. "We need to get ready for Eli."

"Good for you!" says Joe. "We're not sure what to do. You and Dolores have experience, right? Any ideas?"

"You'll want to cover the windows," Paco tells the men. "It helps protect the glass." He looks at a tall tree over their house. "That tree will drop a few branches, and they'll blow around the yard some, but you should be OK. It probably won't fall."

"Probably?" Joe looks up. The tree is right outside Kyle and Ethan's window. His sons often lie in bed and watch squirrels. The little animals chase each other up and down the branches. Now it looks scary.

"How heavy is a tree?" he asks.

"Heavy," says Paco. "But like I said, this tree will drop branches before it falls. Paco points to another tree across the street. "Those fall," he says, "but not always."

"Can it reach our house?" Joe looks at the tall, healthy tree. It has white branches and bright green leaves.

"It didn't fall in the last few hurricanes. Why should it now?" says Paco.

"Anyway, if things get bad, come to our house."

"But you have trees over your house, too!" says Joe.

"If a tree falls on our house, we'll come to your place!" says Paco.

"So you are staying?"

"Yes," says Paco. "We want to be around to help the neighbors. I like to keep an eye on Miss Polly. She lives alone, you know."

"Well, if you are staying, we'll stay," says Joe.

"It's always an adventure," Paco laughs. "Let's get your house ready. I have time. Let me help you. Do you have water and food?"

"Yes," says Joe.

"Candles and flashlights? You'll lose electricity."

Joe nods. "I'll tell Brita. She's going shopping with Dolores later."

"Good. Then we just need wood for your windows."

The three men get in Paco's truck, and he pulls into the street. Paco is turning the corner when he sees Olivia on the sidewalk. Paco stops and rolls down his window, "Hey, Olivia," he says.

Olivia looks up from her phone.

"Hi, Mr. Paco," she says. She looks at Joe and Rashid. Joe nods. Rashid looks the other way.

"Are you and your mother ready for Eli?" Paco asks. "We're off to get some wood. We can get you some."

"Um, I need to ask my mom. We have to go to Dallas. I want to stay here, but she won't let me stay by myself."

"OK, just call if you need anything. We can keep an eye on your place, too."

"Thank you," says Olivia. Then she looks at Rashid again. "Rashid?"

Rashid looks at her. Then he quickly looks away.

"Can you call me?" Olivia waits.

Rashid shrugs, but he does not speak.

"Any time," she says, "I need to talk to you about something."

Paco looks from Olivia to Rashid, but Rashid is silent.

"OK, then," says Olivia. She steps back. Paco says goodbye and drives away. Olivia stands on the corner and watches.

When the men arrive at the parking lot, it is full. Paco stops to wait for a space. A mother and father are putting wood on top of their car. Their two children stand next to them. There are bottles of water in the back.

"We're not the only ones," says Paco.

The family leaves, and Paco parks. Inside, the lines are long. People chat about the storm while they wait to pay. "It's coming around midnight," says a man with three flashlights.

"I'm worried about the animals," says a woman with a box of candles. "We rescued a lot of dogs and cats in the last storm."

It is late afternoon when they arrive home with the wood. The sky is gray and still. The three men work quickly. They put boards over the windows of the yellow house. Then they put away flowerpots and Kyle's small swimming pool.

Down the street in the blue and white house, Dolores and Brita are cooking a green chicken stew. Kyle and Teddy carry toys inside. The boys put blankets over chairs to make a tent. Then they take flashlights inside the tent and pretend there is a storm. Little Ethan plays with dishes on the kitchen floor. The women step over him.

Paco, Joe, and Rashid come over. They put boards over the windows. The boys hear the banging, and they come out of their tent.

"The house is dark!" says Teddy.

"In the daytime!" says Kyle.

The house gets darker and darker. Finally, Dolores turns on the lights.

The men finish and come inside. Dolores puts a big pot of stew on the table. "I always cook a lot before a storm," she says. "It's hard to make food in the dark."

"Or wash dishes," says Brita.

The two families sit down together. While they eat, they watch TV. A reporter is standing next to a line of parked cars. He is talking about traffic on the freeways. People are trying to leave Houston, but there are too many cars. No one is moving. He tells people to stay home if they can.

"I don't like it," says Teddy.

Dolores turns off the TV. "We don't need to watch that," she tells Teddy. "We can play a game instead."

They play a card game, and Teddy wins the first time. Then Kyle wins the second game. Joe keeps checking his phone.

"We should go," he says at last.

They go out on the porch. The sky is black above, and a breeze blows the treetops. The neighbors' houses are covered and dark. Only Jane and Olivia's house has lights. Jane did not cover her windows before she left.

"I guess she was in a hurry," says Dolores.

"Look, she also left some plants on the porch," says Brita. She shines her flashlight on two pots with flowers. "Should we move them?"

They cross the empty street. Brita carries Ethan. Teddy and Kyle hold the flashlights while Joe and Rashid move the pots under the porch stairs.

"Hey," says Rashid. "I found Olivia's phone." He holds up a pink phone.

"She probably dropped it when they left," says Dolores. "I'll text Jane and tell her you have it."

Rashid nods. He hands the phone to Brita. "You take it."

Brita looks at the phone. A message comes up. She reads the message. Then she looks at Rashid. "OK," she says. "I understand."

They walk back across the street. Their footsteps are loud in the quiet night.

"The calm before the storm," says Brita.

"Remember! We're home if you need us," says Paco.

Joe and his family watch their friends. The yellow lights from their flashlights get smaller and smaller. They hear the door open, and Paco and his family disappear inside.

8. Stuck

Olivia sits in the back of Jane's car with two cat carriers. Winken is in one, and Blinken is in the other. The cats are not happy.

"We shouldn't have left," Olivia says.

"Nod will be fine," says Jane. "She's a smart cat. She'll find a safe place, or Dolores will take care of her."

"How do you know?" Olivia frowns.

"We could text, but someone forgot her phone."

"Don't you have Dolores's number?"

"Yes, but it's turned off while I drive."

"Can I just check?" Without waiting for an answer, Olivia takes her mother's phone from the front seat. She turns it on. A message from Dolores brightens the screen.

"Brita has my phone," Olivia says.

"Why does Brita have it?" Jane frowns.

"It was on the steps outside the house. They were moving some plants off our porch."

"They didn't need to do that."

"Well, they did."

Olivia texts Dolores about their third cat, Nod. Then she looks out the window. There is a long line of cars. No one is moving.

"The neighbors are all staying. Why can't we?" she says.

"We don't have to do what every-one else does. We're not sheep," says Jane.

"I need my phone."

"I'm sorry you forgot your phone. But we need to get out of here in the next hour, or we'll have a much bigger problem."

"I didn't forget it! It fell out of my bag." Olivia rolls down the window. She hears voices. People are standing next to their cars and talking.

"You're letting all the cold air out!" says Jane.

Olivia rolls up her window. Winken is crying in her cat carrier.

"I know how you feel," Olivia tells the cat.

"Eat some barbecue," says Jane.

"I'm not hungry," says Olivia.

"Wasn't it nice to see Skip?" Jane tries to change the subject.

"No," says Olivia.

"I don't believe you," says Jane. "He was so cute when he saw you. His face lit up."

"Mom, please stop."

"I can't help it honey." Jane looks at Olivia in the rearview mirror. "You two are so good together. His mother thinks so, too."

"Mom, we broke up."

"Only because he was moving to Europe. Now he's back."

"If you like him so much, you date him!"

"Something is seriously wrong with you, Olivia. You and Skip grew up together. You get along. Don't you want an easy life?"

"First of all, while Skip may be a great guy, I'm not looking for a husband. And second, no. I don't want an easy life."

"What are you talking about? Everyone wants an easy life."

"Not me. I want an interesting life. I want to travel."

"But you can do that with Skip."

"Did you not hear him? He hated Europe. And I'll tell you something else. Skip doesn't have an easy life."

"Everyone has a few problems, honey. What about that boy you are seeing? If you ask me, he's nothing but problems. First, he started a fire. Then he got himself hit by a car."

"I knew it! You always have to say something bad about Rashid. You can't even say his name. *Rashid*. I dare you to say it."

"Olivia, listen to me! I just think Skip is so much healthier for you."

"Mom, I hate to tell you this. I promised Skip I wouldn't, but Skip is not healthy. In fact, he's really messed up."

"No, Skip isn't, but I think you are!" says Jane.

Olivia opens the car door and gets out. She closes the door and walks down the freeway. She hears her mother calling her name.

Olivia turns. "You go to Dallas, mom. I'm going to get my phone."

"Olivia, come back here. You know I can't leave the car!"

"It's OK, mom," Olivia shouts. People stop talking and look at her, but she does not care. "It's only a mile back to the house. I'll stay with the neighbors."

"Olivia!"

Olivia turns and walks between the rows of cars. Jane keeps calling, but Olivia does not stop. A few minutes later, she starts to run.

9. Memories

Later that night, Hurricane Eli blows in. The wind gets stronger and louder. The yellow house shakes. Branches hit the sides and bang on the roof.

"Good thing we covered the windows," says Brita. She and the boys are making beds on the floor of a back room. "We'll sleep here. I want us all to be together."

"This is how we slept when I was little," says Joe. "Do you remember that, Rashid?"

Rashid is standing by the window. He looks at Joe. "Yes, I remember. When we all visited our grandparents, there were about twelve kids. It was fun!"

"Did you sleep on the floor every night?" asks Kyle.

"Yes. Your grandparents' house had only three rooms," says Joe.

"Were they poor?"

"No, it was normal for an old house in the country. We used the same rooms for sleeping, eating, visiting, everything."

"Yeah, they didn't have a separate dining room," says Rashid.

"But it was a great house," says Joe. "It had a beautiful garden with vegetables and fruit trees."

A branch hits the house with a bang. Ethan and Kyle hug their mother. "I have an idea," says Brita. "Your father brought pictures from Syria. Let's look at them."

"Now?" Joe looks at Brita.

"Now is a perfect time. We still have lights."

Joe gets the photo book. Then he sits by Kyle and opens it. Ethan cannot see. He pulls it away. Kyle pulls it back.

"Hang on there." Rashid sits on the other side of Ethan. "I want to see, too."

Brita is in the middle, so Joe gives the book to her, and she opens it. There is a photo of two boys on the flat roof of a small house. They are shaking the branches of a tree. "That's your uncle and me," Joe says. "We were picking fruit, so it was summer."

"We used to sleep on that roof, too," says Rashid.

"I remember, and you liked to tell stories at night. I remember one about some little people living inside the walls of a house."

"You can't live inside a wall," says Kyle.

"Little people can," Joe says. "In Rashid's stories they did."

"But walls aren't that wide," says Kyle.

"Some are," says Joe. "That's how they made houses in the old days."

"Can we go there?" asks Kyle. "I want to see it."

"Maybe someday," says Joe. "When the war is over."

"If it's still there," says Rashid. "I hope so. I always liked that house."

Kyle turns the page. There is a photo of two older boys on motorcycles.

"That's my brother and me," says Joe.

Suddenly, they hear a bang. The room goes black.

"Mommy!" yells Kyle. "I can't see."

"It's OK, honey." Brita lights a candle. "We expected that. We're all safe here."

Joe puts his arm around Kyle's shoulder. Rashid takes a blanket to the door. The wind blows around the house. Branches bang on the roof and the walls.

"I didn't know my dad had a motorcycle," Rashid says after a while.

"He did," says Joe. "But your mother made me promise not to tell you."

"That sounds like her. When was that?"

"When we were in college. We used to ride into the mountains for days. We didn't have a tent. We just took a blanket and some bread."

"So much fun!" says Rashid. "Just like my friend Nabil and me. We did the same. We didn't tell my mom. We said we were staying with a friend, and we'd go out and sleep under the stars."

"Your mother knew," said Joe. "Mona paid your cousin to follow you."

"No!" says Rashid. Then he nods. "Actually, I believe it."

Joe tells more stories about Syria before the war. Then the storm quiets. Brita and the boys fall asleep. After a few minutes, Joe does, too. Rashid listens to their breathing, but he is wide awake.

10. Eli

Miss Polly is watching TV and eating cake when the lights go out. She does not want to go upstairs, so she lights a candle. Then she sits in the dark living room and listens to the wind.

Suddenly, there is a flash of light and a loud crash. Miss Polly screams. Something big and heavy falls on the house. The wind blows in, and Miss Polly can feel the rain hitting her face, hard. She cannot see, but she can hear. Small branches fly through the living room. Glass breaks. She wants to get up, but she cannot.

"Tilly!" she screams. She tries to get up again, but then Tilly jumps on her, and she falls back.

"It's OK, Tilly." The old woman reaches for the dog. Tilly is shaking. Miss Polly holds Tilly and tries to move her legs, but a tree branch is on top of them.

"I guess I won't get to finish my cake," she says. She hears more banging. The tree is still moving in front of her. It is slowly crushing the wall. The wood is breaking, but there is nothing she can do. She is going to get wet. Her sofa will get wet. She will have to buy a new TV.

"Stop barking, Tilly. We'll fix it tomorrow," she tells the dog. Tilly does not stop, and Miss Polly pets her. There is another flash of lightning, and she sees the white tree in the sudden bright light. Its blowing leaves and branches shine for a quick moment. Then it is dark again.

"Well, that's a strange thing," Miss Polly laughs. "We have a tree in the house!"

Miss Polly holds Tilly and waits for the tree to crush her. She feels a strange calm. She closes her eyes and thinks about rain. When she was a girl, she played with her friends in the rain. It was warm and loud, and it filled the river behind her parents' house. She was in love with a boy, then. She remembers his wet black hair and running in the rain. She wants to see him again, but it was a long time ago.

11. The Eye of the Storm

Rashid hears a noise, and it is not the storm. He picks up a flashlight and goes to the front of the house. Someone is banging on the door. Carefully, he opens it and steps back. A small dark shape enters.

"You?" He takes a breath.

"Surprise!" Olivia pushes back her rain jacket. Her hair is wet, and there are cuts on her face.

Olivia smiles at Rashid. "You're mad at me, aren't you?"

"Um, I'm a little confused. But that's not important right now."

"I can explain," she says. "But right now, I need your help."

"What? Out there?"

"It's OK. We are in the eye of the storm. We have a few minutes. Take your flashlight."

Olivia pulls Rashid outside. They go down the steps. Branches cover the ground, but the air is still and dry.

"Look up," says Olivia.

Rashid sees stars. "Cool!" he says.

"But we can't stay. Come on." Olivia pulls Rashid by the hand. "We don't have much time."

"What is it?"

"Miss Polly. A tree fell on her house."

They climb over the fallen branches. The tree crushed the fence, so they climb straight into Miss Polly's yard.

Olivia stops and points her light. A white tree lies across the yard.

"Wow!" says Rashid. Olivia moves the light along the tree to the porch. There are branches and leaves everywhere. They cannot see the roof or the front door.

"Quick! We have to hurry," Olivia says.

"Is she in there?"

"Yes, I'm sure of it. Tilly is barking," says Olivia.

"How did you get here?"

"I came back home. I'll explain later."

"How do we get in?"

"Let's try the back." Olivia takes Rashid around the house. The back door is locked, so they return to the front. Olivia shines her light into the branches. "The windows are broken."

The pair push the branches away. Rashid uses his flashlight to break glass in a front window. They climb in.

"Miss Polly?" Olivia shines her flashlight into the house. Tilly barks.

Olivia and Rashid follow the sound. They find the old woman and her dog on the couch.

"She's stuck under this branch," says Rashid.

"Miss Polly?" Olivia shouts.

Miss Polly's eyes open.

"She's alive," says Olivia. "How do we get her out?"

Rashid shines the light around. Then he goes behind the couch and pulls. It moves slowly. Olivia jumps between the tree and the couch. She moves a branch and frees Miss Polly.

Tilly jumps on Olivia, and she pushes the dog away.

"Hurry," she says. "The wind is coming back."

Rashid carries Miss Polly to the back door. Olivia follows with the dog and unlocks it. They go outside and carefully climb over the broken fence. Olivia moves branches out of the way so Rashid does not fall.

They are almost across the yard when they hear the sound of breaking wood. They cannot see it, but they hear a crash as the tree falls further into Miss Polly's house.

"My poor house," says Miss Polly.

When they get to the yellow house, the front door is open. Joe is standing in the doorway with a flashlight. He steps back when he sees them. "What are you doing out there?"

"You're not going to believe it," says Rashid, "but Olivia just saved Miss Polly's life."

12. Morning

Miss Polly wakes up in a strange room. She sees a window, but it is dark behind the glass. Then she sees a woman with brown eyes and long black hair. It is her neighbor.

"Where's Tilly?" says Miss Polly. She sits up, but when she moves, her body hurts.

"Tilly is fine," says Dolores. "You are fine. You are safe."

"Yes, I can see that," says Miss Polly. "Where am I?"

"You're at Brita and Joe's," says Dolores.

"I don't remember coming here." Miss Polly looks around. There is a blanket over her. Then she remembers the tree.

"The . . . the . . . !" she says and stops.

"Tree, Miss Polly. You've got a big tree in your living room," says Dolores.

"Right, and little animals, too," says Miss Polly. She tries to think of the word.

"Squirrels," says Kyle. He laughs. "Squirrels in the house!"

"Don't laugh," says Miss Polly. "They'll be hard to get rid of."

"Their tree fell down," says Kyle. "They'll need a new home."

"Well, I will too," says Miss Polly. "And I'm not going to live with those animals." Then she laughs. "The squirrels can build new homes. It'll be easier for them. They won't have to talk to the insurance company."

"How is she?" Brita walks into the room.

"She's laughing," says Dolores.

Brita turns to Miss Polly. "I brought you a cup of green tea."

"Thank you," says Miss Polly.

"How do you feel?" Brita asks.

"I have a headache," Miss Polly puts her hand on her head.

"You got a little banged up," says Dolores. "But you are lucky." She tells Miss Polly about Olivia and Rashid. "Olivia was passing by when she heard the crash."

Miss Polly shakes her head. "Young people! They can't do anything without their phones!"

"It's a good thing, too. They rescued you."

Miss Polly smiles. "Where are they now?"

"Outside," says Brita. "They're clearing the streets. As soon as we can get a car out, we're taking you to the hospital."

"I'm not going to the hospital."

"Yes, you are."

"No, I'm not. I'm fine."

"You have a black eye," says Dolores.

"Oh, that's why it hurts," Miss Polly says.

"You also have a few cuts," says Dolores. "But you're lucky. That tree almost killed you."

Miss Polly takes a deep breath and nods. She drinks her tea. "Is Eli gone?"

"Yes. It's morning, and the storm is over."

13. The Street

Rashid looks at Oliva over a pile of branches. "You surprised me. I thought you went to Dallas."

"I changed my mind," Olivia says. "Actually, I didn't. I never wanted to go to Dallas in the first place."
"So you just jumped out of the car and ran down the freeway?"

"Yep. I couldn't stay with my mother."

"That sounds like something I would do."

"Yes, it does." Olivia smiles.
Rashid looks at her. She has leaves in her hair and cuts on her face, but she looks beautiful in the wet gray light.

"That was so dangerous," he says. "A hurricane was coming."

"It didn't matter." Olivia looks at him, "I wanted. . . ."

"Your phone," Rashid finishes her sentence.

Olivia smiles at Rashid, "I wanted to talk to you."

Rashid puts down a branch and looks at Olivia. He feels afraid of her next words. "Couldn't it wait until after the storm?" he asks.

"I didn't want to wait."

"Why?"

"I had to tell you something."

Rashid does not want to hear about Skip. He bends over and picks up a branch.

Olivia moves closer to him. She puts her hand on the branch and slowly takes it away from him.

"I don't know what you heard," says Olivia, "but I think you have this idea that I am seeing someone else."

"Skip."

"Did someone tell you about him?"

"I saw you with him."

Olivia sighs.

"You were holding hands."

"Oh, Rashid," says Olivia. "It's not like that. Skip has problems. I was trying to help him."

"It didn't look like friends."

"Skip has a lot of stress. He's hurting. He's hurting himself, and he needs a friend."

Rashid looks at Olivia. "You're not dating him?"

"No," Olivia reaches up and brushes a leaf from Rashid's hair. "I know him well, and I wanted to help. That's all."

"Oh."

"I didn't mind running through a hurricane. I knew you were upset, and I wanted to explain."

Rashid looks at her. "I was confused."

"Don't be." Olivia takes a step closer. Rashid takes a breath. His heart is beating hard. Then he puts his arms around Olivia, and they kiss.

14. Fruit Tart

The next day, the sky is clear. Shini and Wren are outside the café. They uncover the windows. Shini leans forward and looks through the glass. "It's OK," she says. "No water damage."

Inside, Shini tries the light, but there is no power. The women carry two ice chests inside. It is dark in the silent kitchen, but a little sunlight comes through the high window. Shini opens the walk-in cooler. She puts a flashlight in her mouth so she can carry the ice chest with two hands.

"Here, let me get that for you," Wren laughs and takes the flashlight.

"It's still cold in here!" Shini says. "I'll hand you the fish first. We'll eat that tonight. It's not going to wait for the power to come back."

She works quickly. Soon both the ice chests are full. There are fresh greens, fish, meat, cheese, and berries. Wren finds some ice in the ice machine, and they cover the food. Then Wren sees a fruit tart. "I could eat some of that," she says.

"Right now?"

"Sure," says Wren. "Those berries look yummy."

"OK, we don't have room for it anyway."

Wren reaches for a piece, but Shini stops her. She puts the dessert on a tray. Then she goes to the dining room and gets plates and forks.

"You're serious?" says Wren.

"Do you have other plans?"

"No."

"Then let's do this right."

"Too bad we can't make tea," says Wren.

"Oh, but we can!" Shini holds up some matches. She lights the stove.

"Ah! You are so smart," says Wren.

"It's not that difficult," says Shini. "Now you make the tea. I'll clear a table."

Shini takes the tart to the dining room. It would be easy to eat inside, but the weather is too nice. She puts the tart on the counter and takes a table outside. She brings out chairs and hangs a basket of flowers.

"There," she says. Then she brings out the tart with extra plates and forks.

Wren arrives with the tea. "OK, you're right. It's beautiful day for a tea party." Wren sits and pours tea in their cups. She adds milk and sugar. "We should do this more often," she says.

Shini serves the tart. "Yes, every time we have a hurricane." She thinks for a minute. "You're giving me an idea. Maybe the café should offer an afternoon tea."

"You do make nice desserts," says Wren taking a bite. "But is it a thing? Other restaurants don't have afternoon tea."

"That's exactly why I should do it," says Shini.

Wren looks over Shini's shoulder. "Let's ask Adriana what she thinks."

Shini turns and sees Adriana. She turns back to Wren and frowns. Then she turns back and smiles.

"Adriana, how are you?"

"Oh, you wouldn't believe it. I had the worst night!" Adriana stops and looks around for a chair.

Wren sighs. Then she brings out a chair.

Adriana sits. She looks at the tart. "That looks yummy!" she says.

"What happened?" asks Shini.

"My cat will not come out from under the bed. There are branches all over my yard. I don't have power. And my ice cream is ruined."

"In other words, you are just like the rest of us," says Shini.

"Only we don't have a cat," Wren reminds her.

"Oh, well that makes it easier." Shini pushes the tart to Adriana. "Have some. It'll make up for your ice cream."

"I will!" says Adriana. "I have a lot of time. I can't open my store this week."

"Your life is not so bad," says Shini. She tells Adriana about the tree on Miss Polly's house. "Olivia and Rashid rescued her in the middle of the night."

"And her dog," says Wren.

"Exciting," says Adriana. "But how? I thought Jane was taking Olivia to Dallas."

Shini smiles. "That was the plan, but Olivia changed her mind."

"No!" Adriana puts down her spoon.

"It's true," says Shini. "Olivia walked back."

"By herself?" Adriana looks up from her tart. "In the storm? Jane let her?"

"Well," says Shini. "Olivia didn't ask."

"I see," says Adriana. She leans forward. "Olivia is in love with Rashid."

Wren and Shini laugh.

"Look!" says Wren. Rashid and Olivia are walking down Nineteenth Street. They are holding hands and smiling.

15. Clean Up

The electricity does not come back to Nineteenth Street for a week. People stay home from work. Children play in the fallen trees. Kyle and Teddy make a small house with branches. Little Ethan looks for squirrel nests in the fallen trees.

Neighbors help Miss Polly with her house. Paco cuts branches, and Joe takes them to the street. Rashid and Oliva work inside. There is water on the floor and in the walls. The couch is wet and broken. They carry it to the street. Rashid starts removing the ruined walls. Olivia cleans up the glass. When she walks by Rashid, he stops and puts his arms around her. They kiss.

Miss Polly watches from Jane's porch. She is staying with Jane. She and Tilly are comfortable in a bedroom on the first floor. The cats do not like Tilly, so they stay upstairs. "I don't have young children," Jane says. "It's no trouble." Miss Polly does not argue.

Sometimes Jane takes Miss Polly to appointments. The doctors say the old woman is OK, but they are a little worried about her head.

"My head is fine," she tells the doctor. "It's just a little . . ." but she does not finish. She cannot think of the word.

The doctor nods and looks worried.

"Banged up," says Miss Polly. "See! I can talk."

"Sure, you can," says Jane. She and Miss Polly are old friends. Jane likes taking care of her.

When the work on Miss Polly's yard is finished, Olivia and Rashid join some volunteers from Paco and Dolores's church. They clean up branches. They take damaged furniture and toys to the street. They fix walls.

One day, they take a break. Rashid and Olivia sit and lean against a fallen tree. Olivia puts her head on Rashid's shoulder. Rashid puts his arm around her. Other volunteers look at them and smile.

"I'm glad I met you," says Olivia.

"I'm glad, too!" says Rashid. "I had to travel around the world, but I'm glad I did!"

"It's strange," Olivia says. "But I like the way I feel when I am with you. I think we are the same."

"In some ways," says Rashid.

"Ways that matter," Olivia says. "You make me want to be a better person."

Rashid laughs. "Please tell your mother that!"

"I think she knows," says Olivia.

After the break, they go back to work. Olivia finds a cat hiding in an upstairs bedroom of the house. She brings the cat downstairs and gives it some water. She is petting the cat when she has an idea. She talks to Rashid.

"Sure, why not?" he says.

Olivia texts Skip: *How are you doing?*

Skip texts back: *Not great. I'm in bed.*

Olivia asks: *Doing what?*

Skip replies: *Playing computer games.*

Olivia texts: *You have power?*

Skip texts: *Yes, and I feel bad because we have electricity and no one else does.*

Olivia asks: *Would you like to be useful?*

Skip texts back: *Maybe.*

Olivia says: *Then get dressed and come help us clean houses.*

After a little while, Skip texts: *I'll think about it.*

Olivia frowns*: It feels good to help people, Skip. Here is the address. Come today. You'll feel better. I promise.*

Skip looks at the text. Then he takes off his headphones and goes to change.

Eric
Whitaker

Reuter
Creation

www.ingramcontent.com/pod-product-compliance
Ingram Content Group UK Ltd.
Pitfield, Milton Keynes, MK11 3LW, UK
UKHW031311300325
5228UKWH00026B/86

9 781956 476422